IZZY & OSCAR

Story by
Allison Estes & Dan Stark

Illustrations by
Tracy Dockray

Published by Sourcebooks Jabberwocky, an imprint of Sourcebooks, Inc.
P.O. Box 4410, Naperville, Illinois 60567-4410
(630) 961-3900
Fax: (630) 961-2168
www.jabberwockykids.com

Library of Congress Cataloging-in-Publication data is on file with the publisher.

Source of Production: Leo Paper, Heshan City, Guangdong Province, China
Date of Production: August 2017
Run Number: 5010088
Printed and bound in China.
LEO 10 9 8 7 6 5 4 3

To Saint Goody-Goody Vincent.
—Tracy

For Lucas James, who is even more talented than Oscar, and who makes sure my own arms stay busy in the best possible ways:
throwing the ball, cooking, helping with school and art projects, driving to soccer practice, and especially hugging!
—Allison

To my daughter Lily, who helped with the original story.
—Dan

Call me Izzy. It's only Isabel if I am in trouble.
And the captain is never in trouble.

Well, almost never.

Everybody in the crew already had a pet, except me.

"A real pirate captain has to have a mascot," Flynn said.

A real pirate should also know how to swim. But if you can't…

Just stay out of the water. A clever captain never walks the plank.

"Avast, me hearties! Let's hunt for treasure."

"Aye-aye, Cap'n,"
Sam said.

Right where X marks the spot, there was Oscar. I guess he just splooshed out of the ocean and slithered into town.

"There's your mascot," Flynn said.

I really wanted a pet monkey. But...little octopuses are pretty cute.
"He'll do," I said. "Load him in the jollyboat and set sail for home."

"Izzy, when I said maybe you could get a pet, I meant a *traditional* pet," Mom said.

"Tradition, smagition," I said. "I will teach him to be a good pet."

At first I didn't know what to feed him.

But it didn't take too long to figure it out.

After a while, he would spit out the can.

The crew had lots of helpful suggestions:

"My cat is soft and snuggly to sleep with," Flynn said.

I tried cuddling up with Oscar, but it was hard to sleep squeezed underneath my bunk.

Timber?

"My bird can perch on my shoulder and say 'Shiver me timbers,'" Tia said.

Oscar could perch on my shoulder. Sort of.

"My dog can play Frisbee," Sam said.

So I tried teaching Oscar some tricks:

"Sit!"

"Shake!"

"Scuttle me skippers!"

Oscar wouldn't fetch a ball or the paper.
He brought back other things.

But he did have one really good trick...

Oscar could blend in with anything and totally disappear. I wish I could hide like that. Especially when my mom says *someone* needs to take out the garbage!

Of course, I had to walk him.
He was pretty good on the leash.

Mostly.

Oscar ate a lot. He grew bigger.
So did his octopoop.

"Hey, maybe you could ride him," Sam said.
I took him to the stable and saddled him up.

"Giddy-up, Oscar."

Trying to teach Oscar to be a pet was a lot harder than I expected. And it was really cutting into my treasure hunting time.

"Come on, Oscar. An octopus belongs in the ocean, not with people."

Oscar went camo.

I hunted high and low, but I couldn't find that scurvy octopus anywhere.

"He'll turn up when he gets hungry," Mom said.

Actually, he turned up even sooner...

A traditional pet does not squoosh out black ink all over everything. And your mother.

"Abandon ship!" I ordered.

Oscar spoodled out the door.

SPLASH!

Double uh-oh.

"Help!" Flynn hollered.

"H-e-e-e-e-l-p," I burbled.

Suddenly, I felt something wrap around my waist and jet me to the surface.

"My cat can't do that," Flynn said.

The pool manager came running. Mom too. "Everyone okay?"

"Shipshape!" I said. "Thanks to Oscar." Then I spied Oscar, squiggling away.

"Ahoy, Oscar! Don't go!"

NO
Lifeguard
on duty

And that's how the City Pool got the best lifeguard ever.

And that's how I finally learned to swim.

There is one more thing I learned octopuses are really good at...

Octofacts:

1. When you want to talk about more than one octopus, you can say "octopuses," "octopi," or "octopodes."

2. Octopuses are very intelligent. They can solve problems, learn, use tools, and they have both short- and long-term memory. They even seem to play!

3. The smallest octopus is the tiny Californian Octopus, which is only 3/8 inch to an inch long. The largest is the Giant Pacific Octopus, which can grow to be more than 30 feet long and weigh over 100 pounds.

4. Octopuses are invertebrates—they have no bones at all. Because of this, octopuses can make themselves nearly flat and squeeze through the thinnest cracks.

5. An octopus can camouflage itself, using special pigment cells in its skin, to look exactly like whatever it wants to hide near. If you put an octopus on a black-and-white checkerboard, it can even manage to imitate that.

6. Octopuses communicate by changing color—when they are scared, they may turn white, just like some people do.

7. When an octopus needs to make a quick getaway, it can squirt out black ink to blind whatever is after it and use a quick burst of jet propulsion to escape: at speeds up to 50 mph!

8. Octopus means "eight-foot." An octopus has eight arms, with 240 suckers on each arm—that's 1,920 in all. It uses its arms and the suckers to catch crabs and to pull open the clams and other shellfish it likes to eat. An octopus can even taste things with its arms. (Imagine having tongues all over your fingers...) The arms are not tentacles—tentacles are found on squid, jellyfish, and other creatures, and may sometimes have one sucker right at the tip.

9. If a predator gets ahold of an octopus's arm, it breaks off. Then the octopus can escape. The arm will grow back (regenerate) in 6-8 weeks.

10. Octopuses have two eyes that look almost like human eyes. They can see very well in the deep water where they live, and have an excellent sense of touch. But they seem to be completely deaf.

11. An octopus has three hearts and blue blood!

12. Octopuses hatch out of eggs and they have sharp beaks, but they are not birds. They are cephalopods.